D1372604

By Tracey Corderoy

Illustrated by Kate Leake

NEVER say NO to a Princess!

The little princess wore a big **sparkly** tiara. She slept in a big **sparkly** bed.

Her big **sparkly** wardrobe was bursting with **sparkly** dresses and her toy box was filled with big **sparkly** toys.

You see, the little princess got everything she wanted
but nothing ever seemed to make her smile.

"Ice cream!" she shouted.
"I want ice cream now!
And it had better be good or else . . . I'll cry!"

"Quick!" said her daddy (who was busy being King).

"Or else she'll cry!"

So ice cream after ice cream was brought from the royal kitchens, but the little princess heaved a great big sigh . . .

"Too **sticky** . . .

too **drippy** . . .

yuck – too **pink!**" she exclaimed. "And look – you've forgotten the sprinkles!"

"Ponies!"
bellowed the little princess.
"I want ponies now! And make them good or else . . . I'll cry!"
"Quick!" said her mommy (who was busy being Queen).
"Or else she'll cry!"

So pony after pony was led from the royal stables,
but the little princess simply shook her head.
"Too **frisky**… too **twinkly**…
yuck – too **sweet!**" she cried.

"And that one doing
ballet is a show off!"

Then, one morning, at breakfast-time,
a big green dragon flew by . . .

"Dragon!"
yelled the little princess.
"I want that dragon NOW!
Get it! Catch it!
Now, now, NOW!
Or else . . . I'll cry!"

"Quick!" said
the royal servants.
"Or else she'll cry!"

swish

Swish, swish, swish, went the royal nets but the dragon just wouldn't be caught.

So the little princess tossed back her head, took a deep breath . . .

...and **cried!**

By lunchtime a river of twinkling tears gushed through the big sparkly palace . . .

By dinnertime it was an ocean . . .

And, by bedtime, the palace went . . .

pop!

Whoosh went the gurgly water
as it swept the little princess
far, far away from home . . .

FAR FAR AWAY

She found herself all alone in a gloomy wood.
Her tiara was bent. Her dress was torn.
She had never been less sparkly.
"I want my mommy and daddy!"
sniffed the little princess.

Twoo

Squeak

Just then, she heard a **swhoosh!** in the dark night sky. The air above her head grew warm. And there, swooping down through the twinkly stars, was . . .

. . . the dragon!

"Dragon!" bellowed the little princess.
"Take me to my mommy and daddy!"
The dragon raised an eyebrow. "What's the magic word?"
The little princess thought for a moment. "Oh, yes," she said.
"Take me to my mommy and daddy NOW!"
"That's not the magic word," said the dragon.
"Fine," said the little princess. "I'm going to cry!"

And she did.

The dragon dried her tears with one blast of hot air from his nose.

Then he swished off into his cave and shut the door.

SLAM!

The little princess was puzzled. Crying usually worked perfectly! She wondered what the magic word could be.

Then she remembered a word she'd heard a long time ago.

She tiptoed up to the dragon's cave and tapped on the door.
   "Will you t-take me to my m-mommy and d-d-daddy, PLEASE?"
      shivered the little princess.

"Certainly!" smiled the dragon. "But first we need to get you warm and dry."

The dragon lit a roaring fire
and they huddled in the orange glow,
until the little princess felt much better.

"Time to go home?"
said the dragon.
"Yes, please,"
said the little princess.

So back they flew

through the **starry** night.

When the little princess awoke, the dragon was gone but her mommy and daddy were **SO** pleased to see her. "Oh – but darling . . ." gasped the Queen. "We don't have **any sparkly things** for you!"

The Royal Footman coughed politely and handed her a catalogue.

"Your Majesty's favorite," he said with a bow.

"Sparkly Things for Princesses!"

"What would you like?" beamed the King.

"Necklaces?

Carriages?

Sparkly shoes?"

But the little princess didn't look very happy.

"I'd like to invite a **friend** to play, please," said the little princess.

"A **friend?**" said the King.

"A **friend?**" said the Queen. "But there aren't any other little princesses for miles around!"

"This is a **special** friend," said the little princess.

She wrote an invitation in her
very best handwriting . . .

. . . and a royal servant
set off to deliver it.

The little princess's special friend wasn't quite what the King and Queen were expecting and his table manners left a lot to be desired.
But, as they ate their sparkly tea, the King noticed something strange.

"Do you think," he said to the Queen, "our little princess looks different?"
The Queen peered through the royal binoculars.
"Heavens!" she gasped.
"You're right! Is she . . . ? No!"

"Yes!"cried the King. "She is! She's smiling!"

And the little princess

kept on smiling all day long!

First published in 2012 by
Alison Green Books
An imprint of Scholastic Children's Books
Euston House, 24 Eversholt Street
London NW1 1DB
A division of Scholastic Ltd
www.scholastic.co.uk
London – New York – Toronto – Sydney
Auckland – Mexico City – New Delhi – Hong Kong

Text copyright © 2012 Tracey Corderoy
Illustrations copyright © 2012 Kate Leake

ISBN 978-1-4351-4970-0

Manufactured in Malaysia
Lot #:
10 9 8 7 6 5 4 3
May 2015

All rights reserved.
Moral rights asserted.

For Eve, with love – T.C.
For my very sparkly cousin, Tala – K.L.